Ten Tales of Coyote

Lynne Garner

Ten Tales of Coyote
Copyright © Lynne Garner 2017
Published by Mad Moment Media
www.madmomentmedia.com

Lynne Garner has asserted her right under the Copyright, Designs
and Patent Act 1988 to be identified as the author of this work.

ISBN 978-1-9996807-1-8

Mad Moment Media is a trading name of Nyrex Limited
Cover illustration and design by Debbie Knight

DEDICATION

For Debbie
for your creative inspiration

CONTENTS

INTRODUCTION

I remember watching Wile E. Coyote cartoons as a child and believing he was a character created by Looney Toons. At the time I had no idea they were drawing on a long tradition of trickster stories enjoyed for generations by the first peoples of America. I stumbled on the 'real' Coyote stories whilst researching for my first collection of Anansi the Trickster Spider stories and knew then I had to retell them.

In the original stories he's not the Wile E. Coyote who invents elaborate traps that always fail to catch his archenemy, the Road Runner. He is a character with many 'faces.' In some he is a creator and a problem solver. In others, he is a teacher who highlights the dangers of bad behavior such as greed, lust and deceit. In some he is a trickster who uses his cunning and quick wits to trick others or get himself out of a sticky situation, whilst in some stories he is a mixture of all these different 'faces.'

Traditionally Coyote appears as a male and is generally anthropomorphic. If the storyteller describes him then he is described with coyote-like features such as a pointed face, a tail, claws and fur. In some stories the storyteller doesn't give a description and allows the reader to create their own image of him.

The original Coyote tales were an oral tradition, so had never been written down. Thankfully this changed when it was realized this long oral tradition was being lost due to the influence of the vast numbers of Europeans who were immigrating to America. Folklorists, many supported by the American Folklore Society and other institutions such as the Smithsonian, were given grants to enable them to undertake 'field trips'. During these trips they documented not only the myths and legends of the native population but also their traditional beliefs and way of life.

As they talked to the elders of tribes and those who still remembered life before the 'white man' the folklorists discovered Coyote was more than just a character in a story. George Amos Dorsey noted in his book The Mythology of The Wichita (published 1904) that an elder and many of his generation believed the myths without question. It didn't matter how puerile or ribald they might seem. He respected the lessons they gave and identified them with the stories told by the 'whites' about Christ, for both he and Coyote lived many generations ago, and appeared in this world to better the lot of mankind.

George Amos Dorsey also noted that parents who belonged to the Wichita tribe used the Coyote stories as a way of teaching their children. They would invite an old man, who they believed had led a good life, to tell Coyote stories to their children, so they could learn important life lessons.

Traditionally Coyote tales were only told during the winter months. It was customary (and still is for those who follow the old ways) for the elders to bring out the stories in November and put them away when the snow melted, usually some time during February or March. However, some would put Coyote stories away when they saw the first snakes as they came out of hibernation. Those that followed this custom also believed that snakes would visit anyone who read the stories during other months.

It is not only important when Coyote stories are shared but also how they are told. Storytellers believed they would be given a sign the day after they shared a story. This sign would tell them how good or bad their story-telling was. For example, if the next morning was bright and started with a light mist then their story telling had been good. But if the next day was excessively cold then their story telling had been poor.

My hope is you enjoy my retelling of these stories and you show respect to the tradition they represent by sharing them only during the winter months. However, if you do share them outside of these months please remember to also share that traditionally these stories are for the winter.

Lynne Garner, September 2017.

"Spring is the time of year when it is summer in the sun and winter in the shade."

Charles Dickens (1812 – 1870)

COYOTE, BEAR AND THE FOUR SEASONS

When the earth was first created there were four seasons: spring, summer, fall and winter. Now, long, long ago Bear decided that because his favorite seasons were winter (he just loved to sleep) and spring (he loved the smell of the spring flowers) he decided he'd catch summer and fall, keep them in a large clay pot and only get them out when he needed them.

This meant if Bear decided he wanted winter to last six months (which is fine if you hibernate like Bear) and spring to last six months, then he could. Sadly, this wasn't good for the other animals, as they never knew when the seasons would change.

•

Now one day during a very cold winter Coyote was trudging through the snow looking for something to eat. His stomach gave a huge, long rumbling growl. "At this rate I'm going to have to eat the snow," he mumbled.

Suddenly, as Coyote walked under a large fir tree, he was showered with snow. He looked up and saw Squirrel looking very thin and sad.

"Squirrel, are you all right?" Coyote asked.

Squirrel burst into tears.

"Squirrel, please come down and talk to me," Coyote called up to Squirrel.

"No, you'll eat me," replied Squirrel. "I can hear your stomach growling from here."

"I promise not to eat you," replied Coyote, who didn't like to see Squirrel so upset.

"Promise?" asked Squirrel, looking down from the safety of the branch.

"I promise," replied Coyote.

Squirrel scurried along the branches, leaping from one to another until she reached Coyote.

"What's the matter?" asked Coyote again.

"My store of nuts is almost empty," replied Squirrel. "I don't have enough to last the winter and as Bear has taken summer and fall I don't know when I can stock up again."

"That is a problem," replied Coyote.

"I'm not the only one," said Squirrel. "Many of the other animals are struggling to survive. We need the four seasons, not just winter and spring."

Coyote sat in the snow and scratched his ear with one of his large back paws. "Let me see what I can do," he said, after a short pause.

"Really?" asked Squirrel. "You'll get the four seasons back for us?"

"I'm Coyote," replied Coyote. "That's what I do."

Coyote then got up, shook the snow from his fur and slowly walked home.

•

The next day Coyote woke from his slumber, stretched, then looked in his cupboard. He shook his head; it was totally empty.

"I'm going to have to visit Bear and have words," he said to himself.

When Coyote reached Bear's den all he could hear was snoring.

Coyote sighed. "Of course, he's hibernating." Coyote went to walk away then turned around. "No, I promised Squirrel I'd help her and the other animals. I'll have to hope Bear isn't too angry when I wake him up."

Coyote knocked on the door, but the snoring continued. Coyote knocked again, louder this time, but Bear still slept on.

"Well, there's only one thing for it," said Coyote.

Coyote took a deep breath, lifted his head and began to howl. He howled and howled for all he was worth.

Finally, Coyote heard the snoring stop, the thud of Bear's large paws on the floor and a long, noisy yawn.

Coyote knocked on the door again and stood back. Coyote knew what Bear was like when he was grumpy and Bear was often grumpy when he first woke up.

Bear's front door slowly creaked open. "What do you want?" he growled.

"Can I come in? It's very cold," asked Coyote.

"Didn't you know I was sleeping?" asked Bear.

"Sorry, Bear, but it's very important," replied Coyote.

Bear gave a long, deep sigh and stood back to let Coyote

in. "Make it quick. I want to go back to bed."

Inside Coyote looked around to see if he could see where Bear had hidden summer and fall.

"What do you want?" asked Bear, stretching and scratching his armpit.

"We need summer and fall back," replied Coyote.

"That's what you woke me up for?" growled Bear. "No, I'm not going to let everyone have them. I'm going back to bed."

"But we need the four seasons," said Coyote.

"Get out!" shouted Bear, pointing at the door. "Get out!"

Coyote decided it wasn't a good idea to make Bear angrier, especially when he was still inside Bear's house.

So Coyote decided to leave. Just as he reached the door Coyote noticed two large clay pots on a shelf. One had the word 'Summer' written on it and the other had 'Fall' written on it.

Coyote smiled to himself. He'd had an idea.

•

Over the next few days Coyote visited his relatives and asked if they'd help him. Being family, they all said they'd be happy to help. Well, they would, wouldn't they? You always help family.

•

A few days later Coyote sat near Bear's house and took a deep breath. He lifted his head and began to howl. He howled and howled for all he was worth. After a little while Coyote's family joined in and the air was filled with a chorus of howling.

Finally, Coyote heard the snoring stop and the thud of Bear's large paws on the floor. "Coyote, stop that noise at once!" shouted Bear. But Coyote and his family continued to howl.

Bear shouted again, but Coyote ignored him.

"I'll make you stop!" shouted Bear. The door flew open and Bear threw a large pot at Coyote. Coyote quickly jumped to one side and the pot hit a tree root. It smashed open and honey started to slowly drip onto the snow.

Coyote sat down again, took a deep breath, lifted his head and began to howl. He howled and howled for all he was worth. Coyote's family joined in and the air was filled with a chorus of howling.

"Right!" said Bear.

He went inside, picked up another pot and came back outside. Standing in the snow, Bear threw the pot at Coyote, but Coyote quickly jumped out of the way. The pot smashed on a small rock jutting out of the snow. But much to Bear's annoyance Coyote and his family continued to howl.

"Now I'm getting really angry!" shouted Bear, who went inside to get another pot. When he came outside again Bear threw the pot at Coyote who quickly jumped out of the way. The pot landed with a soft thud in the soft snow.

Coyote sat down again, took a deep breath, lifted his head and began to howl. He howled and howled for all he was worth. Coyote's family joined in and the air was filled with a chorus of howling.

"OK, you win!" shouted Bear, who went inside and this time picked up two pots. Bear walked back to the door and threw the pots at Coyote. Again Coyote jumped out of the way. As the pots arced through the air they bumped into one another and smashed into a thousand pieces. To Coyote's delight, he felt a warm summer breeze on his face, followed by the sweet smell of ripe fall berries. As good as his word, Coyote had made Bear give back the two seasons to the other animals.

• • •

COYOTE, BEAR AND THE FOUR SEASONS

"Now there were stars overhead, hanging like frozen spears of light, stabbing the night sky."

Neil Gaiman (1960 – present)

COYOTE PLACES THE STARS

One night Coyote was enjoying a walk when he came across the four wolves and their friend, Dog. The five animals were sitting on the edge of a cliff staring into the night sky.

Coyote was a little confused because they weren't staring at the glorious moon, but at the blackness of the skies. You see, no one had come up with the ideas of stars. So the only two things you'd see in the sky was the moon or the sun. Sometimes, if you were lucky, you could see both at the same time.

Coyote wanted to know what they were staring at, so he sat next to the largest wolf. "What are you looking at?" he asked.

"Oh, nothing," replied the largest wolf.

"But you must be looking at something," said Coyote.

"We're just looking," said the smallest wolf.

Although Coyote knew they must be staring at something, he couldn't see what it was, so he shrugged his shoulders and left them still staring into the night sky.

•

The next night Coyote found the four wolves with their

friend, Dog, in the same spot. This time Coyote sat next to the second largest wolf.

"What are you looking at?" he asked.

"Oh, nothing," replied the second largest wolf.

"But you must be looking at something," said Coyote, this time a little annoyed.

"We're just looking," said the smallest wolf.

Although Coyote knew they must be staring at something, he couldn't see what it was, so he shrugged his shoulders and left them staring into the night sky.

•

The next night Coyote found the four wolves with their friend, Dog, still sitting in the same spot. This time Coyote sat beside Dog.

"What are you looking at?" he asked.

The four wolves looked at Dog and waited to see if he would answer Coyote.

"We can tell him," said Dog. "Coyote's clever and he may be able to help."

Eager to find out what they were staring at, Coyote said, "I'm sure I can help if you tell me what you're staring at."

The smallest wolf pointed into the sky. "If you look very closely, just there, you can see two creatures sitting in the sky," the smallest wolf told him. "They're there every night but we can't work out what they are."

Coyote looked into the sky and concentrated on the spot the five animals were staring at. The wolves and Dog were right: there were two animals sitting in the sky.

"We just can't make out who or what they are," said

Dog.

"We've all suggested something but none of us can agree," the largest wolf added.

"We could go up there and take a closer look," suggested Coyote.

"How could we do that?" asked Dog.

"We've tried to come up with a way but we've all failed," said the middle wolf.

"I'm sure I can think of a way," replied Coyote. "Meet me here next time the clouds are low."

"All right," said the wolves and Dog in unison.

•

A few nights later the clouds were low and covered most of the sky and, as promised, Coyote met the wolves and Dog. However, this time he was carrying a fine bow with lots and lots of arrows.

"What are they for?" Dog asked.

"Watch," said Coyote.

Coyote stood on the edge of the cliff. He took the first arrow, placed it on the bow, aimed and fired it into the nearest cloud. The arrow shot up into the air and, to the surprise of the wolves and Dog, it stuck into the cloud.

The wolves and Dog gasped.

"I've never seen that before," said the smallest wolf. "How did you do that?"

"I'm Coyote," replied Coyote.

Coyote then took another arrow, and fired it into the air. This time the arrow stuck into a slightly higher cloud. Coyote took another and another and another. Soon he'd fired all the arrows into the clouds.

"A ladder," said Dog surprised.

"How clever!" said the largest wolf.

"Let's climb," said Coyote, standing back to let the wolves and Dog climb the ladder of arrows.

Everyone climbed and climbed and climbed. Finally, they reached the place where the two creatures were living.

"They're grizzly bears," said Dog.

The four wolves crept forward, closely followed by Dog.

"I think I'll stay here," said Coyote. He'd fooled Bear and didn't know if his cousins had heard about his trickery and would be angry with him. As the four wolves and Dog slowly crept forward the two bears turned around and stared at them.

"They'll tear you apart!" shouted Coyote. But the two bears sat down and simply looked at their visitors.

The largest wolf sat down, the second largest wolf sat down and soon all the animals were sitting and facing one another.

The bears sniffed the cold night air. The wolves and Dog sniffed the cold night air. None of the animals moved. They simply watched each other whilst Coyote watched from a safe distance. As he watched, Coyote muttered to himself, "That makes a very nice pattern. It would be lovely if everyone could see it."

Time ticked by as the two bears, four wolves and Dog continued to watch one another, each wondering what to do next.

Coyote noticed the sun peeking over the horizon. I think

I'll go back. I'll leave everyone here. They all seem happy, Coyote thought.

Coyote quietly walked back to the ladder and started to climb down, pulling the arrows out as he went. To his delight, he found climbing down was far quicker than climbing up. When he reached the ground, Coyote looked up, but the sky was filled with large white fluffy clouds which hid the animals.

Coyote yawned and thought, I'll come back tonight to find out if everyone is still there.

•

That night Coyote walked to the edge of the cliff, sat down and looked up. The sky was clear and the moon was shining bright. He smiled when he saw the four wolves, two bears and Dog still sitting in the same place.

"I'll think I'll call them stars," said Coyote to himself. "And the pattern they make I'll call the Bear."

As Coyote stared at the new pattern in the sky he smiled as an idea started to take shape. "I think I'll make more stars and more patterns and give each one their own story."

So, Coyote spent the next few nights placing more stars in the night skies and making more stories. When he finally finished filling the skies with stars he visited Meadowlark.

"Meadowlark, have you seen the night sky filled with stars?" he asked her.

"I have," replied Meadowlark. "It's beautiful."

"I want you to tell everyone it was my idea to fill the skies with patterns made from stars. I also want you to tell them the patterns have stories and if they ask me I'll tell them the stories."

Meadowlark nodded and said, "I'll tell everyone and I'm sure they'll want to hear your stories, Coyote."

"Thank you," said Coyote, who returned to his den for a well-deserved sleep.

• • •

Note:

The collection of seven stars that feature in the story has had many names including 'The Bear', 'The Dipper' (US) and 'The Plough' (UK).

The 'First Peoples' of Canada call it the 'Fish Star' after the fishing cat and when slavery was legal in America many slaves who attempted to escape to Canada (where slavery was illegal) called the stars 'The Drinking Gourd'.

There are other versions of this story that feature either a mother bear and her cubs or several hunters tracking a bear.

COYOTE PLACES THE STARS

*"Coyote is always out there waiting,
and Coyote is always hungry."*

Navajo Proverb

COYOTE, THE DANCING MICE AND
THE OLD ELK SKULL

"What a fantastic night!" said Coyote, looking up and admiring the full moon and twinkling stars. Just then a gentle breeze picked up and Coyote sniffed the cool night air. He tipped his head to one side and listened. "Is that music and dancing I can hear?" he asked himself.

Coyote continued to listen and was soon tapping his paw and gently swishing his tail along to the beat of the music. "I think I'll find out who that is," he said as he stood up and stretched.

Coyote listened for a moment to make out where the music was coming from. As he listened, the sound of the music grew louder and softer as the night's breeze ebbed and waned.

Coyote slowly walked in the direction of the sound, looking and listening as he went. But try as he might he couldn't work out exactly where the music was coming from. Coyote was just about to give up when he suddenly saw a small flickering light coming from the middle of a large bush. Coyote edged forward, crouched down and looked under the bush. "Well, I never," he said. "I've never seen a party being held inside an old elk skull before. Those mice seem to be having a wonderful time."

Some of the mice were dancing around and around, their tails curling in the air as they swished and swirled. Others stood in a large circle clapping their paws and tapping their feet, whilst a small band was playing drums, wooden flutes, bells and rattles.

As Coyote watched he let out a small sneeze. Each and every mouse froze and slowly looked in Coyote's direction. Their eyes became wide and a few of them gasped.

A small mouse with a rip in his ear shouted, "RUN!"

In a hushed voice Coyote said, "Please don't run. I was enjoying watching you."

One of the largest mice crept forward and said, "But you're Coyote. You'll eat us."

Coyote shook his head. "I promise not to eat you if you let me watch you dance," he said.

"We don't trust you," said another mouse, who was missing the tip of his tail. "We know how you love to play tricks."

"I won't eat you, I promise," Coyote assured the mice.

"As long as you promise," said the large mouse. "Then we'll let you watch." The large mouse then nodded at the band, who began to play again. Although a little scared, the other mice started to dance, but they kept an eye on Coyote, just in case he changed his mind.

As he watched, Coyote's tail flicked in time with the music and his paw tapped gently on the soft ground. Coyote then decided he wanted to see more so he slowly crept nearer and nearer until finally his head was inside the skull. As he watched Coyote started to feel a yawn creeping up on him. The urge grew stronger and stronger until he couldn't hold it in any longer. As his mouth opened the mouse with the ripped ear shouted, "RUN! Coyote's going to eat us."

The instruments clattered to the ground as the band got up and ran. In a flash the mice had disappeared into the night.

"Oh well," said Coyote. "Might as well find myself a little snack." Coyote then tried to pull his head out of the skull. But he found he was stuck. "No! no!" he shouted.

Coyote shook his head from side to side, but the skull wouldn't budge. Coyote pawed at the skull, but it still didn't move. Coyote hit his head on the ground, but the skull just wouldn't come off.

"What am I going to do?" he asked himself. "I can't stay like this."

Coyote thought and thought, but he just couldn't come up with an idea. Finally, he decided he'd go down to the river to try and get a drink. When he reached the riverbank he noticed a small campfire on the other side. In the dim flickering light he could see two human figures sitting by the fire, which had a large pot hanging over it.

"Mmm, that smells good," Coyote said, licking his lips. Just then his stomach grumbled. "Perhaps I can help myself to a little food when they go to bed."

So, still wearing the old elk skull, Coyote crept forward so he could watch and wait. As he watched, the lovely smell became stronger, which made Coyote's stomach grumble even more. Coyote became stiff, so he wiggled a little to get more comfortable, but as he did he snapped a small twig.

"A monster!" shouted the little boy.

"A spirit of the night," said the old man. "If we give him some food perhaps he won't hurt us."

Coyote's ears pricked up (well, as much as they could inside the old elk's skull). Not wanting to miss the opportunity of an easy meal, he paddled across the river, his stomach still grumbling and gurgling.

"Quickly, give the night spirit some food," the old man told the boy.

The boy spooned some food from the pot into a round bowl. With his eyes wide and his muscles tense, the boy slowly crept towards Coyote and put the bowl on the ground. He then quickly backed away.

Coyote stood as tall as he could and he raised his head. He tried to howl, but he could only mumble, "Yaoomph, yahoomph, yahumph."

The boy, very scared, hid behind the old man.

Coyote walked forward and sniffed the food. His stomach grumbled and gurgled again. The sound seemed to scare the boy even more.

Coyote turned his head to one side then to the other as he tried to eat through a small opening at the front of the old elk skull. Finally, he managed to lap the food with the boy and the old man watching from a safe distance.

When he'd finished, Coyote nudged the bowl towards them.

"The night spirit wants more," said the old man. "Give it to him."

"But there's not much left," said the boy.

"A full spirit is a happy spirit. Would you prefer an unhappy hungry spirit?" asked the old man.

The boy shook his head and filled the bowl again, then put it on the ground in front of Coyote.

Just as Coyote finished his third bowl the sun started to peek over the horizon.

"Why," said the old man, with relief in his voice. "It's not a night spirit at all. It's just a tricky coyote wearing an old elk's skull."

The old man looked around, bent down and picked up a large stone.

"Be gone, you scoundrel!" he shouted as he threw the stone at Coyote. CRUNCH!

The stone hit the old elk skull right between the eye sockets. CRACK!

The old elk skull broke in two. CRASH!

The old elk skull fell to the ground.

Coyote shook his head and howled for joy.

"You don't scare me!" shouted the old man, as he picked up another large stone. "Be gone, you trickster, be gone."

"Thank you," howled Coyote, who then turned, ran across the river and disappeared into the bushes.

• • •

"I am clever enough to know that I am clever."

Mervyn Peake (1911 – 1968)

COYOTE, MOUSE AND ELK

Coyote was on his normal early evening walk when he came across something very strange. Jack Rabbit and his family, Skunk, Prairie Dog, Fox, Raccoon and Chicken were standing on the very edge of the prairie. They were all staring into the middle and talking in hushed voices.

"What's going on?" Coyote asked Skunk

"Shhh," replied Skunk. "You'll annoy Elk."

"What do you mean, I'll annoy Elk?" asked Coyote.

Skunk pointed to the middle of the prairie. "Elk's told everyone that the prairie is his and no one else can use it," replied Skunk.

"And we daren't try our luck," whispered Jack Rabbit. "Elk is in a really bad mood this evening."

Coyote looked out into the middle of the prairie where Elk was lying on a small hill, enjoying the evening sun.

"Who is he to tell us what we can and can't do?" asked Coyote, a little annoyed.

"He's Elk," replied Skunk.

"I'm not having this," replied Coyote. "The prairie belongs to everyone, not just Elk."

"What are you going to do?" asked Jack Rabbit.

"I'm not sure," said Coyote. "But I'll come up with something. I always do."

Just then Coyote saw Mouse scampering around the base of the hill. "I think I have a plan," said Coyote, who smiled as he disappeared into the long grass.

"What do you think he can do?" asked Skunk.

"I'm not sure," Jack Rabbit replied, shrugging his shoulders. "But Coyote always manages to get what he wants."

•

Later that night Coyote found Mouse nibbling on a seed.

"Hello, Mouse," said Coyote.

Mouse dropped the seed and began to run away.

Coyote quickly pounced on Mouse and held him between his large paws.

"Please, please don't eat me!" Mouse pleaded.

Coyote could feel Mouse trembling. "Don't worry, I'm not going to eat you," he said. "I need your help."

Mouse stopped trembling. "My help?" he asked. "How can I help you? Everybody knows how clever and cunning you are."

"Even I need a little help sometimes," said Coyote, with a smile. "I saw you in the middle of the prairie earlier. Didn't you know Elk has claimed it as his own?"

"Oh yes," replied Mouse. "Being small sometimes has its advantages as he never notices me."

"How do you get so close?" asked Coyote.

"There's an old badger sett that stretches under the prairie. The badgers moved out many summers ago," replied Mouse. "There are miles and miles of tunnels. I use them all the time."

"And you can get to the middle of the prairie where Elk is sitting without being seen?" asked Coyote.

"Oh yes," replied Mouse.

"Will you show me the way?" asked Coyote.

"As long as you promise not to eat me," replied Mouse.

"I promise not to eat you," Coyote assured Mouse. "Can you meet me tomorrow at this time?"

"I can," replied Mouse.

"See you then," said Coyote, who then disappeared into the long grass.

•

The next day Coyote found Jack Rabbit and his family, Skunk, Prairie Dog, Fox, Raccoon and Chicken all standing on the very edge of the prairie again. They were all talking in hushed voices.

Coyote smiled and checked the direction of the wind. "Good," he said to himself quietly so the other didn't hear. "It's blowing in the right direction."

He joined the other animals and looked out to the middle of the prairie and saw Elk sitting in the middle again.

"Well, he is very brave," said Coyote in a very loud voice. "I'm not sure I'd sit there on my own."

"Why?" asked Jack Rabbit.

"Haven't you heard about the ghost that lives under that hill?" Coyote almost shouted.

Elk twitched his ears and looked in the direction of

Coyote and the other animals.

"What ghost?" asked Jack Rabbit's youngest kit.

"I can't believe you haven't heard about it," said Coyote. "If you're alone it'll come out of hiding and jump on you. If you're lucky you'll get away, but…"

"What, what?" asked the little kit.

"You're far too young to know what it does," replied Coyote, ruffling the little kit's fur.

"Please, please tell me," the little kit pleaded.

Coyote checked Elk was listening and replied, "No, I don't want to give you nightmares." Coyote then disappeared into the long grass.

•

That afternoon Coyote found Mouse in the same spot nibbling on a large juicy berry.

"Good evening," said Coyote.

Mouse jumped, dropped the berry and looked up at Coyote with wide eyes. "You promised you wouldn't eat me," he said.

"I did," said Coyote, with a smile. "But only because you agreed to show me the way to the middle of the prairie."

"Then follow me," replied Mouse.

Soon Coyote and Mouse were looking into the blackness of the old badger tunnels.

"Are you sure you remember the way?" asked Coyote. "It looks a bit of a squeeze and I wouldn't want to get stuck."

"I'm trusting you not to eat me," said Mouse. "So you must trust me."

Coyote nodded and followed Mouse into the darkness of the tunnels. On and on the two walked deeper and deeper into the tunnels.

"Ouch," mumbled Coyote for the sixth time. "I'm going to have to have words with the badgers. Their ceilings are very uneven."

"Are they?" asked Mouse, who'd never had that problem.

Eventually a small ray of light could be seen at the end of the tunnel.

"At last," said Coyote, with a sigh. "I didn't think we were ever going to get to the end."

"You're going to keep your word now I've helped you, aren't you?" asked Mouse.

"I'll keep my word, but I need you to do one more thing for me," replied Coyote.

"What's that?" asked Mouse.

"Run out onto the prairie shouting as loudly as you can that the ghost is chasing you," Coyote told Mouse.

Mouse looked a little confused, but decided it would be a good idea to do as he was asked.

Mouse took a deep breath and ran out of the hole into the fading light.

"HELP, HELP!" he shouted. "The prairie ghost is chasing me. He's going to eat me."

Whilst Elk watched Mouse, Coyote slowly and quietly crept up behind Elk.

"I can't see…" Elk said.

"BOO!" shouted Coyote as loudly as he could.

Elk looked around with wide eyes. "What…"

Thankfully Elk didn't recognize Coyote because he was covered in mud and bits of root.

"AN ELK… I LOVE ELK MEAT!" shouted Coyote.

Elk stood up and ran as fast as he could. When he reached the edge of the prairie the animals got out of his way.

"The ghost is after me!" he screamed. "It's going to eat me."

Jack Rabbit and his family, Skunk, Prairie Dog, Fox, Raccoon and Chicken looked into the middle of the prairie. And who should they see sitting on the small hill in the middle of the prairie? Why, Coyote, of course.

"He's a clever fellow," said Raccoon.

"I'd not want to be him when Elk discovers he's been tricked," clucked Chicken.

"Can we go onto the prairie now?" asked the little kit. "Can we? Can we?"

Jack Rabbit nodded and the little kit hopped onto the prairie and began to nibble at the delicious grass as Coyote watched from the top of the small hill.

• • •

COYOTE, MOUSE AND ELK

"The bold are helpless without cleverness."

Euripides (480BC – 406BC)

COYOTE HELPS MOUSE FOOL OWL

Coyote was sitting on the top of the small hill in the middle of the prairie watching the other animals enjoying their day. Jack Rabbit was keeping an eye on his kits as they played a game of tag. The ground squirrels were busy nibbling on the first seeds of fall. Chicken and her chicks were pecking at the ground, creating small dust clouds. And Owl was showing her owlets how to swoop, glide and hover.

"I can see why Elk wanted to sit here," said Coyote. "It's a lovely spot."

Just then Coyote's paw began to itch. He sighed and scratched it on the ground, but it continued to itch. This time he gave his paw a little nibble, but it still itched. He looked down and to his surprise he saw Mouse staring up at him. Mouse quickly stepped back.

"You promised you wouldn't eat me," said Mouse, his eyes wide. "You'll keep your promise, won't you?"

"I will," replied Coyote.

Mouse let out a long sigh of relief.

"Why have you come to see me?" asked Coyote.

"I… no, we," said Mouse, "need you to talk to Owl for us."

31

"Us?" asked Coyote.

"My family and friends," said Mouse. "Owl hunts us day and night. We never know when we have to hide or when it's safe to come out."

"What do you want me to ask her?" asked Coyote.

"We want her to choose when she's going to hunt," said Mouse. "All we need is for her to decide if she's going to hunt by day or at night."

"I'll try," said Coyote. "But Owl doesn't listen to anyone."

"But you're Coyote," said Mouse. "You can do anything."

"I am, and you're right. When do you want me to get her to hunt?" asked Coyote.

Mouse thought for a moment. "At night," he said.

"Let me see what I can do," replied Coyote.

"Thank you," said Mouse who then went down the hill, into the badger tunnels and vanished into the darkness.

"How am I going to get Owl to hunt just at night?" Coyote asked himself. Coyote then smiled one of his smiles. The smile everyone else dreads because it means Coyote had come up with one of his ideas.

"Oh, Coyote, you're clever! Such a simple idea" Coyote muttered.

•

The next day Coyote sat on top of the small hill and watched as Owl glided over the prairie. Every so often she hovered, then dropped like a stone and disappeared into the long grass. Moments later she'd reappear, shaking her head because her talons were empty.

"Owl!" shouted Coyote as she swooped over his head. "You'll catch more if you hunt at night."

Owl circled around and landed almost silently next to Coyote.

"I catch more if I hunt during the day," said Owl. "My owlets are growing fast and they're always hungry."

"I've seen them," said Coyote. "You're a good mother. But if you hunt at night and rest during day you'll catch more."

"I'm sure you're wrong," replied Owl.

"Perhaps we should have a competition," suggested Coyote. "You spend all day tomorrow hunting mice and I'll spend all night tonight hunting. Whoever catches the most mice wins and can choose when the other hunts."

"OK," said Owl. "We'll meet here at sunset and see who's the winner." She then flew off as silently as she'd landed.

•

A little later Coyote came across Mouse, who was carrying the largest hazelnut Coyote had ever seen.

"I've had a talk with Owl," Coyote told Mouse.

"What did she say?" Mouse asked.

"We're going to have a competition," replied Coyote.

"A competition?" asked Mouse.

"We're going to see who can catch the most mice," replied Coyote.

Mouse dropped the nut he was holding. "What?" he squeaked. "That's not what we wanted."

"Don't worry," said Coyote. "I have a plan."

"What is it?" asked Mouse, picking up the large hazelnut he'd dropped.

"Owl will be hunting all day tomorrow," Coyote told Mouse. "So you need to tell your family and friends to hide."

"I can do that," said Mouse.

"I also need you to tell them to trust me," said Coyote.

"Why?" asked Mouse, becoming a little nervous.

"When I meet Owl I need every mouse to lie on the ground around me pretending to be dead," Coyote said.

"I'm not sure they'll do that," said Mouse, shaking his head.

"Then I can't win the competition," said Coyote.

"I'll try my best," said Mouse, who then turned around and scampered into the long grass.

•

Just before the sun began to set Coyote was sitting on top of the small hill in the middle of the prairie. Suddenly he noticed a mouse emerge from the badger hole, followed by another, then another and another. Soon an army of mice was scampering up the hill, making their way to where he was sitting. Soon he was surrounded by the largest mischief of mice he'd ever seen.

Mouse stepped forward. "We're here," he said.

"I can see," replied Coyote, with a smile of his face.

"I promised everyone you wouldn't kill us," said Mouse.

"I won't. I just need their help to fool Owl," said Coyote. "All they need to do to is lie down and not move, not even a whisker."

The mice looked at one another, then looked at Mouse.

"It's the only way," Mouse told them, as he lay down next to one of Coyote's large round paws.

The mice looked at one another, then at Mouse, then at Coyote. One or two shook their heads, shrugged, then lay down. Then one by one the other mice lay down as well.

A few moments later Owl fluttered down and landed next to Coyote. She looked around. "I've been hunting all day and didn't catch a single mouse," said Owl. "How did you catch so many?"

Coyote just smiled.

"Well, it's obvious you've won," said Owl. "So you can choose when I hunt."

"I think we should both hunt at night," said Coyote.

"Really?" asked Owl, amazed. "I thought you'd keep the best hunting time for yourself."

"As you can see, there is enough for both of us," said Coyote. "And you do have your owlets to feed."

"I'd heard you were wise," said Owl. "Thank you." She then looked around. "I don't suppose I could take…?"

But Coyote stopped her. "I'm sorry, Owl, but I promised to help Snake. She has so many snakelets to feed."

"Mmm, plump snakelets," said Owl as she spread her wings and flew silently across the prairie.

As soon as she was out of sight Mouse jumped up, quickly followed by his family and friends.

"Thank you, Coyote," said Mouse. "I didn't think you'd

get Owl to agree to hunt just at night."

"As you said, Mouse, I'm Coyote and I can do anything I put my mind to. Now you'd better take cover because it's Owl's time to hunt."

The mice looked at one another and within a blink of an eye they were gone.

• • •

"It is a fool who thinks he cannot be fooled."

Joey Skaggs (1945 – present)

COYOTE, FOX AND THE FISHING HOLE

Fox shivered as he plodded through the deep snow towards the lake. He shivered and blew on his paws. "When will this winter end? It feels as if spring will never arrive," he said.

When he reached the lake he was surprised to see Coyote sitting in the middle of the lake on the ice. He was surrounded by fish with his tail dangling over the edge of a hole.

Fox's stomach grumbled. "Mmm, that pile of fish looks good," he muttered as he licked his lips.

Just then Coyote noticed Fox was watching him from the shore.

"Helloooo!" he shouted. "The fish must be hungry today. They've not stopped biting."

Fox's stomach gave another long, rumbling growl. "I wonder if Coyote will share?" he asked himself. "Only one way to find out."

So, Fox carefully stepped onto the ice and, one slow step at a time, he walked and slid his way to Coyote.

"Hello," he said when he finally reached Coyote. "What a lot of fish."

"I know. I can't believe my luck," replied Coyote. "Beaver made this breathing hole this morning and I couldn't let it go to waste."

Fox's stomach gave another low, rumbling growl. "I'm sorry," he said, a little embarrassed.

Coyote smiled and said, "I've more than enough fish. You're more than welcome to have a go yourself."

Fox tried to hide his disappointment. He really wanted Coyote to share. He didn't want to catch his own.

"I'll even leave you my fish bait," said Coyote. "Just place some on the end of your tail. As you can see, the fish seem to love it."

"Thank you," said Fox.

"My pleasure," replied Coyote, as he pulled his tail out of the water and shook it dry. Coyote then picked up his fish, handed Fox a small bag of bait and slowly and carefully walked back to the shore.

"I hope he left some fish for me to catch," said Fox, as he spread some bait onto the end of his tail and dipped it into the water. Within a few moments Fox felt a tug on the end of his tail.

"Oh... oh!" he shouted in excitement. He quickly pulled his tail out of the hole. As the cold water sprayed in all directions a fish plopped next to him. "It worked!" said Fox, astonished.

Fox quickly spread more fish bait on the end of his tail and popped it into the cold water. Again, within minutes Fox had caught another two fish. "Oh, I am looking forward to my tea tonight," said Fox as he spread a little more bait on the end of his tail. But this time Fox waited and waited. As he waited he watched Deer as she came down to the shore and tried to break the ice with her hoof, so she could have a drink. He watched Eagle as he soared on the wind above him.

Fox then realized how cold he was getting. "Brrr," he muttered. "Perhaps three fish are enough." But as Fox tried to pull up his tail he discovered the hole had closed up and his tail was stuck fast. He pulled and pulled, but it just wouldn't budge.

"Help! Help!" he shouted. "Help! help!" But no one heard him and soon the sun was getting very low in the clear winter sky.

"What am I going to do?" Fox asked, as he breathed on his paws to try and keep them warm.

Just as the sun began to disappear below the horizon Fox was sure he heard a noise under the ice.

"Who's there?" he shouted.

Fox then heard a rasping sound. Scared, Fox tried to pull his tail out of the ice. The rasping sound carried on and this time Fox was sure he felt something brush the end of his tail. "Oh my," he said as he pulled harder on his tail.

The rasping sound carried on. Fox pulled his tail with all his might and POP, out it came.

"Ouch!" said Fox as he fell back on the ice with a bump.

Fox lay on the ice nursing his bruised head and frozen tail when suddenly Beaver's head popped up out of the hole.

"Well, hello, Coyote, I did tell you…" He stopped when

he saw Fox.

"You told him what?" snapped Fox.

"That if he didn't keep chipping at the edges of the hole it would close up and his tail would become caught," replied Beaver. "Didn't he tell you?"

"No, he didn't!" replied Fox.

"I'm sure he meant to," said Beaver, who then disappeared beneath the ice.

"I'll, I'm going to…" said Fox, picking up the fish and then slipping and sliding back to the shore.

•

The next day poor Fox was still suffering with his numb tail. "I'm sure Coyote forgot to tell me on purpose," he said as he carefully placed his tail in some warm water.

"Oh, that's nice," he said with a slow sigh.

As he sat with his tail in the warm water Fox decided he'd visit Coyote. So when he could feel his tail, he walked to the lake. When he reached the shore he found Coyote coming off the ice with an armful of fish.

"Hello there," said Coyote. "How was the fishing?"

"The hole closed up and trapped my tail," replied Fox, trying to keep his temper. "If it hadn't been for Beaver I'd still be there."

"Really?" replied Coyote, with a sly smile on his face.

"You forgot to tell me on purpose, didn't you?" Fox almost shouted.

Coyote smiled. Fox growled. Coyote stopped smiling. Fox growled again and leapt forward. Coyote quickly stepped to one side and started to run. As he ran Coyote looked over his shoulder and shouted, "It was only a joke."

"It wasn't funny!" shouted Fox. "Coyote, you'd better run fast."

Just then Coyote had an idea. He swerved and disappeared into the long grass.

"You won't lose me that way!" shouted Fox, close on Coyote's heels.

Soon Fox came to the edge of the prairie. He stopped. He couldn't see Coyote anywhere. He sniffed the air and smiled. "I may not be able to see you, but I can smell those fish," said Fox as he followed the fishy scent.

Soon he reached a large tree. The first time I've met a tree that smells of fish, he thought. Fox then noticed a large hole hidden among the roots.

"Coyote, come out," Fox growled.

Fox heard a shuffling, then the sound of fish being dropped on the floor.

"You're trapped," shouted Fox. "So come out now!"

Inside the old gnarled tree Coyote muttered so Fox couldn't hear, "Oh, Fox, when will you realize you're not as clever as me?"

"Coyote, don't ignore me. I know you're in there!" Fox shouted.

Coyote smiled, then muttered, "Fox, as my way of saying sorry, I'll leave you a fish or two." Coyote then slipped out of the smaller hole at the back of the tree.

"Coyote, Coyote, if you don't come out, I'm coming in!" Fox shouted again.

Coyote smiled. "Fox, I hope your tail's better soon."

And with that Coyote slipped unseen through the long grass and back home to his den.

• • •

COYOTE, FOX AND THE FISHING HOLE

"They are most cheated who cheat themselves."

Danish proverb

COYOTE AND TURTLE OUTWIT BEAVER

Whilst on his evening ramble Coyote found Turtle sitting and staring into the middle of the river.

"Evening, Turtle," said Coyote. "What are you watching?"

Just then a small bubble popped to the surface, quickly followed by a second, slightly smaller bubble.

"Beaver's up to his old tricks," replied Turtle, who then gave a long, slow sigh. "He and Otter are having a competition to see who can hold their breath the longest."

"Is there a prize?" asked Coyote, also watching and waiting for the next bubble to float to the surface and pop.

"The usual," replied Turtle. "Whoever loses has to leave this part of the river. Beaver has decided it's not big enough for everyone to live in and he's claimed it's his."

"Who do you think will win?" asked Coyote.

"I hope it's Otter, otherwise it'll be me next," said Turtle with another huge sigh. "I'm the only one left. Beaver has managed to beat everyone else."

Just then a small bubble floated to the surface and gave a little pop. However, this time it was quickly followed by an eruption of water as Otter exploded to the surface, gasping for breath.

"Did… did I… win?" spluttered Otter, looking around trying to find Beaver.

"Oh well, that'll be Otter leaving then," said Turtle, looking down at the ground and shaking his head.

"He must be cheating," said Coyote. "Otherwise he couldn't have beaten everybody on the river."

Turtle lifted his head and smiled. "Well, if he can cheat, so can I," he said.

"Would you like some help?" asked Coyote.

"Yes, please," replied Turtle, a broad grin now replacing his frown. "I'm sure between us we can beat him. It'd be lovely to have everyone back. The river's been far too quiet."

Just then Coyote's stomach gave a little grumble. "That's my cue to find myself some supper," he said. "Let's meet tomorrow and see if we can come up with a plan to beat Beaver."

"I'll be here sunning myself in my favorite spot," replied Turtle.

"See you then," said Coyote, as he ducked under a bush and disappeared into the long grass.

Just as Coyote's tail disappeared among the thick green blades of grass Beaver swam over to Turtle. Turtle knew what was coming. "I suppose you want to suggest a contest," he said.

"How did you know?" asked Beaver.

"Clever, I suppose," replied Turtle.

"Then how about tomorrow afternoon?" suggested

Beaver.

"Late afternoon," Turtle said. "I need some time so I can tell everyone to come and watch me beat you."

Beaver laughed, then replied, "Late afternoon it is, then." He then slipped his head under the water and swam to the other side of the river.

•

The next morning Coyote found Turtle warming himself in the glorious morning sunshine.

"Good morning," said Coyote. "Are you ready to show Beaver just how clever we are?"

"I am," replied Turtle. "Just as you left last night he came over and challenged me."

"How long do we have?" asked Coyote.

"Until late this afternoon," replied Turtle.

Coyote scratched his head as he started to think. "We need something you can hide behind or under and still be able to breathe."

"There's a canoe a short distance upstream," said Turtle. "Perhaps we can use that."

"That should do it," replied Coyote. "We can put it among the reeds, so you can hide behind it whilst I sit in it and watch for bubbles. When I think he's about to give up I'll let you know and you can swim back out to the middle."

"Great idea," said Turtle. "I'll meet you there." Turtle then quickly slipped into the water and began to swim up-river.

Coyote followed the shore and soon found the small

canoe bobbing in the water. Coyote chewed on the rope and as it frayed the boat rocked from side to side. Within a few moments the rope snapped and the boat began to drift into the middle of the river. Just then Turtle's head popped out of the water. He grabbed the end of the rope in his mouth and slowly began to drag it to the reeds.

"See you there!" shouted Coyote.

Soon the boat was in among the reeds and Turtle had worked out where he was going to hide.

"I'm going to tell everyone to come down to the shore and watch you beat Beaver," said Coyote. "I'll see you later this afternoon."

Word soon spread that Beaver and Turtle were going to have a contest and a group of animals had gathered on the shore. Along with Turtle and Coyote there was Goose, Heron, Kingfisher, Otter, Fox and Raccoon. All were eager to see Turtle win.

"Why are you all here?" asked Beaver angrily as he climbed out of the water.

"We're here to see who wins," said Coyote.

"It'll be me," said Beaver pompously.

"I wouldn't be so sure," said Jack Rabbit, as he hopped down to the water's edge and joined the others.

"Shall we get on with it?" asked Turtle. "I'm eager to invite everyone back to the river."

"Phuph!" Beaver snorted.

"I think I'll go and sit in that canoe," said Coyote. So as Beaver and Turtle swam out into the middle of the river Coyote walked over to the canoe and settled himself down.

"On the count of three," said Beaver. "One, two, three."

Beaver and Turtle gulped down a huge breath of air and slid under the water.

Beaver sank to the bottom of the river as he always did, closed his eyes, concentrated and slowly started to count. Turtle, however, swam as fast as he could to his hiding-place behind the canoe.

Everyone on the shore watched the water. Time ticked by and everyone began to become a little concerned. Then a large bubble floated to the surface and gave a loud pop. Then a few smaller bubbles broke the surface. As agreed, Coyote gently tapped on the bottom of the canoe. Turtle took a deep breath and swam out into the middle of the river. He then started to blow out small bubbles, so it looked like he, too, was also running out of breath.

Eventually Beaver wasn't able to hold his breath any longer so he swam to the surface as quickly as he could. As he broke the surface he coughed and spluttered. He then looked around for Turtle. "Where is he?" he asked breathlessly.

The only answer he got was the cheers from everyone standing on the bank.

Under the water Turtle heard the cheering and knew it was time for him to come up. He quickly swam to the surface, burst through the water and gasped for breath.

"There's no way you could've beaten me!" shouted Beaver.

"Well, he did!" shouted Coyote, from the canoe. "Now it's your turn to leave the river."

"No, wait," said Turtle. "Beaver, you're welcome to stay on two conditions."

Although Beaver didn't want to agree he also didn't want to leave. "What are they?" he asked.

"Firstly, everyone who had to leave can return," said Turtle.

Beaver nodded.

"Also, you have to make one of your famous dams so the water levels rise. That way there'll be room for everyone. Oh, and you are to look after it for as long as you live in the river," said Turtle.

Beaver nodded again.

Goose, Heron, Kingfisher, Otter, Fox, Raccoon and Jack Rabbit cheered and clapped. Some even jumped into the water.

Coyote simply smiled and disappeared into the long grass.

• • •

"There is a foolish corner in the brain of the wisest man."

Chinese proverb

COYOTE AND THE STRANGER

"What a lovely evening," said Coyote as he snuck out of his den. "I think I'll sit and watch the sun set over the river."

Soon Coyote was sitting by the water's edge enjoying the last of the sun's warmth on his fur. Coyote looked down and watched his reflection as it rippled and twinkled in the fading light.

"Mmm," he muttered. "What mischief can I get up to tonight?"

Just then he heard a human voice from the other side of the river. Looking in the direction of the voices, he saw two young boys. They were standing talking, both holding a fishing spear in one hand and fish in the other.

Just then one of the boys noticed Coyote.

"Look, there's a coyote!" he shouted, pointing to where Coyote was sitting.

"And look, there's another one!" said the second boy.

Coyote then noticed a stranger standing a little way downstream by the water's edge.

The two coyotes watched the boys as they bent down and picked something up from the riverbank. They watched as the boys raised their arms and threw a stone each. The first stone missed the stranger, but the second stone hit Coyote squarely on the nose.

"Ouch!" winced Coyote, who then shouted to the stranger, "Quick, run!"

The two coyotes turned tail and retreated into the cover of the bushes and grass. When they felt safe, they stopped running and stood facing one another.

"Hello, stranger," said Coyote. "I've not seen you before. Where are you from?"

"I've travelled from the North country," the stranger told Coyote. "This looked like a good place to find some food and water."

Coyote smiled, as he now knew how he could make some mischief. "What are you?" he asked. "I've never seen a creature like you before."

The stranger looked a little puzzled. "Why, I'm a coyote, like you," he replied.

"No, you're not," said Coyote.

"Of course I am," replied the stranger. "Didn't you see our reflections when we by the river? We're exactly the same."

"I did," said Coyote. "You may think we look the same, but the rest of the world doesn't."

"I don't understand," said the stranger. "How can we be the same, but be seen differently? You're wrong."

"Trust me," said Coyote. "We're different and I can prove it."

The stranger looked confused. "Of course we're the same; it's plain for everyone to see."

"We may look the same, but you're not a coyote," replied Coyote.

The stranger sighed. "My friend, I'm a coyote. Our ears and mouths are the same. Our eyes and nose are the same. Our fur and tail are the same. We could be brothers from the same litter."

Coyote shook his head. "I'll prove to you the world doesn't see you as a coyote," said Coyote, trying to hide a smile.

"How?" asked the stranger.

"Meet me by the water's edge tomorrow, just before the moon and the sun change places," replied Coyote. "Then I'll prove I'm right and you're wrong."

"I'll see you then," replied the stranger and the two coyotes went their separate ways.

•

The next day, as agreed, Coyote went down to the water's edge. Enjoying the last of the day's warmth on his fur, Coyote quietly sat and watched his reflection as it rippled and twinkled. Soon he noticed the reflection of the stranger sitting beside him.

"Look, reflections don't lie," said the stranger. "Can't you see you're wrong? We're the same in every way. You look like my brother and I look like yours."

"We may look the same, but I'm Coyote and you're not," replied Coyote.

Puzzled, the stranger looked at the reflections as they gently rippled. "Can't you see how we're the same?" asked the stranger again.

Coyote was amused by the stranger's confusion. "Stranger, if you're patient, I'll prove I'm Coyote and you're not."

"I just don't see how," asked the stranger.

"Just wait and you'll see," replied Coyote, who then added, "I'm just going to walk along the river bank a short distance. Stay there and I'll be back."

The stranger watched as Coyote moved along the shore and sat down. He shook his head. He simply didn't understand how Coyote could possibly prove he wasn't a coyote when it was so plain he was.

Just then the stranger heard human voices. Alarmed, he glanced in the direction of the voices. He saw the two young boys from the night before. They were both carrying a spear and some delicious-looking fish.

"Look, there's a coyote!" shouted one of the boys, pointing to where Coyote was sitting.

"And there's another one," said the second boy, who pointed to the spot where the stranger was sitting.

The two coyotes watched the boys as they bent down and picked something up from the riverbank. The coyotes watched as the boys raised their arms. This time they knew what was going to happen, so they got up, turned tail and disappeared into the cover of the long grass and bushes.

When they felt safe, Coyote and the stranger stopped running and stood facing one another.

"See?" said the stranger. "Didn't you hear those boys shout that there were coyotes?"

"That's not what I heard," replied Coyote, looking a little

disappointed.

"I heard them as clearly as I hear you," said the stranger. "They called us coyotes."

Coyote smiled, then replied, "No, my friend, they called me a coyote. You, they called *another one!*"

• • •

"Beware of the half-truth. You may have gotten hold of the wrong half."

Anon

COYOTE AND TIP BEETLE

Coyote was lying on a large, weather-worn rock watching the sun's rays as they turned the low wispy clouds yellow, orange and red. What a wonderful sight, he thought. Then, out of the corner of his eye, he noticed a movement. He looked over the edge of the rock, tilted his head and concentrated on the roots of the old oak tree. A pair of antennae appeared between the roots that stretched out across the dusty ground. They were quickly followed by a black head and long winged shell. "Hello, Tip Beetle," said Coyote, a smile creeping across his face.

He continued to watch as Tip Beetle scuttled across the scorched earth, leaving a small trail of dust behind her. She was heading to a large bush that was surrounded by faded flowers, which had dropped earlier that day.

"Oh my, a banquet," he heard Tip Beetle say as she reached the first wilting flower.

I can have some fun here, thought Coyote. He slowly stood up, jumped down from the rock and sauntered over to the bush.

"What a wonderful smell," he said, sniffing the last few flowers on the bush. He then pretended to sneeze and, as he did, he blew some of the wilted flowers along the track.

"Watch what you're doing!" shouted Tip Beetle.

Coyote pretended to sneeze again, blowing more of the once pretty flowers along the track. "I'm sorry," he said.

"I was going to eat those," said Tip Beetle angrily. "Now I'll have to travel miles to reach them."

Looking at where the flowers lay, Coyote replied, "That's not miles."

"It may not be for you, but it is for me," said Tip Beetle.

Coyote pretended to sneeze again and the faded red flower Tip Beetle had been eating rolled along the track.

"Whoops, I'm sorry," he said. "I didn't mean to."

Coyote then turned and, as he walked along the track, he chuckled.

Tip Beetle, overhearing, said, "Right, I'm not going to let you get away with that!" and she scurried over to the wilting flowers she was going to enjoy eating.

•

The next night as Tip Beetle came out of her resting place she smiled. The sky felt restless and the fresh-smelling wind was blowing in small gusts, swirling around and around.

"I recognize that feeling and smell," she said. "My shell's telling me there's a storm coming. I can use this to teach Coyote a lesson."

As she feasted on a freshly-fallen flower she kept an eye out for Coyote. Just as he rounded the large, weather-worn rock she placed her head to the ground and tipped her bottom towards the sky. She looked as if she was doing a headstand.

"What's that you say?" she asked. "Really, are you sure?"

"Who are you talking to?" asked Coyote, seeing Tip Beetle with her head to the ground.

"The spirits who live underground," she replied. "They're chatting away this evening. I've found it's worth to listening to them. They're very wise."

"I can't hear them," said Coyote.

"Place your ear as close to the ground as you can and listen very hard," Tip Beetle told him.

Coyote put his ear on the dusty earth and listened.

"A storm, you say?" said Tip Beetle. "Thank you for the warning. I'll find a new place to sleep."

"I still can't hear them," said Coyote, a little annoyed.

Tip Beetle stood up and stared into Coyote's eyes. "You're not listening hard enough," she said. "I've learned to listen to them. If they tell me a storm's coming, then a storm's coming."

Coyote looked up. All he could see were thin wispy white clouds slowly drifting across the sky. "I'm not sure they're right this time," he said.

"Well, I'm going to find a safe place to rest tomorrow," said Tip Beetle. "You can ignore the spirits if you want, but I'm not going to." She scurried off towards some freshly-fallen petals.

•

The next day, just as Tip Beetle said the spirits had predicted, a fierce storm rolled over the land. The fine white clouds of the night before were replaced with low, threatening grey clouds. The sky filled with flashes of lightning and the land shook under the rumbles of thunder. Bushes were torn from their roots. The old oak tree that had stood for many, many years now lay broken on the soaked earth.

By late afternoon the storm had passed and Tip Beetle darted out of her resting place. She found a puddle in a small dip in the rock and enjoyed a refreshing drink. She had just finished drinking when she noticed Coyote trotting towards her. She smiled and quickly scuttled across the rock and dropped to the ground. She placed her ear to the ground and stuck her bottom into the air.

"Really?" she said. "I thought you were happy living underground."

As Coyote reached Tip Beetle he said, "The spirits were right."

Tip Beetled pretended to jump. "Coyote, don't do that. You know what happens to anyone who makes me jump."

Coyote took a small step back and wrinkled his nose. He knew about Tip Beetle's secret weapon. He'd seen her cover Mouse, a couple of Jack Rabbit's bunnies, Fox and Prairie Dog's youngest pup with her smelly spray. He also knew they now all called her 'Stink Beetle' behind her back.

"Were you listening to them again?" Coyote asked.

"I was," she replied. "But their voices are muffled and I'm having to listen very, very hard."

"What are they saying?"

"If you keep quiet, I'll listen," said Tip Beetle. Sticking her bottom into the air and putting her ear on the damp ground, she pretended to listen.

"I'm sure he didn't mean to," said Tip Beetle. "He can't help it."

"What are they saying?"

"Ssshhh!" Tip Beetle said, waving one of her legs at Coyote.

Coyote bent down and placed his ear on the damp earth.

"But his paws are so big," said Tip Beetle. "I'm sure he didn't mean any disrespect."

"I can't hear any voices," said Coyote.

Tip Beetle lifted her head. "How could I warn you about the storm if they hadn't told me?" she asked. "Do you think I'm making it up?"

"No, not at all," said Coyote, taking a small step back. He didn't want to find out what it was like to be sprayed by her.

Tip Beetle placed her ear to the ground again and pretended to listen. "I look forward to meeting you," she said, "and I'm pleased I'm not Coyote."

Tip Beetle raised her head and looked straight into Coyote's eyes.

"A friendly warning," she said. "If I were you, I'd stay away for a while."

"Why?" Coyote asked.

"The spirits' home is full of water, so they're moving above ground for a while," she replied. "But ..."

"But what?" asked Coyote.

"Well," said Tip Beetle. "They're fed up with listening to your huge paws as you follow the track. So, they're going to play a trick on you."

"How do they know it's me?" asked Coyote.

"You think you travel lightly on those paws but, trust me, you don't. They said they've heard every thundering step you've taken along the track," said Tip Beetle.

"When are they coming?" asked Coyote, a little worried.

"Soon, very soon," replied Tip Beetle.

"When will they return home?" Coyote asked.

"Not until the rains stop," Tip Beetle said.

"Thank you, you're a true friend," said Coyote. "I'll make sure I stay away."

Coyote slowly turned around and, as quietly as he could, he walked along the track and out of sight.

Tip Beetle smiled as she watched Coyote walk along the track. Now for a lovely freshly-fallen flower, she thought, looking around and seeing a few lying nearby.

• • •

Note:

The Tip Beetle is the folk name for the Western Pinacate Beetle (Eleodes). It's also known as the 'Stink Beetle' because of the foul-smelling substance it sprays when it feels threatened. Some also call it the 'Clown Beetle' because when it puts its head to the ground and its bottom in the air it looks like it's standing on its head.

"I can do things you cannot, you can do things I cannot; together we can do great things."

Mother Teresa (1910 – 1997)

COYOTE AND THE SMALL RAY OF SUNSHINE

Coyote was lying on the small hill in the middle of the prairie, watching two of Jack Rabbit's babies playing a game of tag, when he heard a rustle in the dry grass. He looked down and standing between his paws was Mouse.

"Hello, Coyote," said Mouse.

Coyote smiled as he remembered how Mouse had helped him teach Elk a lesson about bullying.

"Hello, Mouse. What are you up to?" asked Coyote.

"Collecting seeds for winter," Mouse replied. Mouse then looked at the fading sun as it painted its colors across the sky. He gave a long, slow sigh. "I sometimes wish we had the summer fire from the sun, so we could keep warm during the winter nights."

"That would be nice," agreed Coyote.

Mouse then said goodbye and disappeared into the long grass. Watching the grass gently move as Mouse wove in and out of the stems, Coyote had an idea. Mmm, all we need is a little ray of sunshine, Coyote thought. He then smiled and said, "I'd need a little help."

•

So, the next day when Coyote saw Mouse he told him he wanted to hold a meeting.

"What's the meeting about?" asked Mouse.

"Well, you gave me the idea," said Coyote.

"Did I?" asked Mouse, looking a little confused. "What idea?"

"To steal a small ray of sunshine from the sun to keep us warm at night," replied Coyote.

Mouse smiled, then asked, "Where and when?"

"Just before sunset on the small hill," replied Coyote.

"I'll spread the word," said Mouse, who then scurried off to tell everyone about the meeting.

•

Later that day Coyote was resting on the small hill daydreaming and enjoying the feeling of a full belly when he was startled by the sound of large flapping wings. He turned his head and found Eagle was sitting beside him, ruffling her feathers.

"Good evening, Coyote," she said. "Mouse told me about his idea and how you have a plan."

Coyote was just about to tell her his plan when he noticed Chipmunk and Squirrel standing, wide-eyed and nervous, at the bottom of the small hill.

"Come on up," Coyote said. "We won't eat you."

"You promise?" asked Squirrel, looking at Eagle.

"We promise, don't we?" said Coyote, looking at Eagle.

Eagle nodded, the sun reflecting on her fine feathers.

Coyote jumped when he heard Mouse's voice beside him. "It's all right, he keeps his word."

Chipmunk and Squirrel slowly walked up the hill and sat near, but not too near, Coyote and Eagle.

"I'm sure I could steal a small ray of sunshine on my own, but it's easier when friends work together," Coyote told them.

"What's your plan?" asked Eagle.

Coyote explained how he planned to steal a small ray of sunshine just as the sun set.

When he finished Eagle nodded her head and said, "That might just work."

"We will need a little luck and just the right evening for it," Coyote said.

"You make it sound so easy," said Squirrel, twitching her tail.

"Together it will be," said Coyote. "So, you'll help me?"

Eagle, Chipmunk, Squirrel and Mouse nodded.

"Then I'll see you tomorrow by the old Joshua tree," said Coyote.

•

The next day Coyote, Eagle, Mouse, Chipmunk and Squirrel met as planned.

"Everyone knows what to do?" Coyote asked.

Eagle, Chipmunk, Squirrel and Mouse nodded. Then Chipmunk, Squirrel and Mouse scurried off in different directions.

Coyote looked up and smiled. The sun's rays looked like long thin fingers as they filtered through the white, low-hanging clouds, covering the ground with slowly-moving shadows.

"We couldn't have a better evening for it," said Coyote. He then looked at Eagle, who nodded, spread her wings and almost silently rose into the sky.

Just then a small ray of sunshine broke through a tiny gap in the clouds above them and turned shadow into light.

"That one!" said Coyote, pointing.

Eagle flapped her huge wings and gracefully flew higher and higher. As the clouds slowly drifted across the sky the small ray of sunshine shimmered across the land. Eagle flew faster and chased the small ray of sunshine. The gap in the cloud started to shrink and so did the ray of sunshine. Eagle held her feet in front of her, grabbed the ray and twisted. There was a sharp splintering sound as the end of the ray of sunshine broke off.

As Eagle turned, it felt as if everything had slowed down and there wasn't a sound. Eagle gulped. Perhaps this wasn't such a good idea after all, she thought. She headed towards the other animals on the ground below her. As she flew, she began to feel her talons warming from the fire trapped inside the small ray of sunshine.

"Hurry!" shouted Coyote.

Eagle looked over her shoulder and saw the sun's rays chasing her. Not a good idea at all, Eagle thought, as she beat her wings harder.

"Drop it to me!" shouted Coyote.

Eagle swooped down and dropped the small ray of sunshine into Coyote's paws. Coyote quickly felt the warmth of the fire locked inside the small ray of sunshine. He then realized the sun and her rays were now chasing him. As Coyote ran he tried to keep to the shadows so the sun couldn't touch him. Just as he reached Chipmunk he felt the tip of his tail becoming warm. The warmth became a glowing heat, then the heat began to sting. Coyote looked over his shoulder and saw the tip of his tail had turned white. As Coyote continued to run he could feel his legs beginning to get tired and he knew he had to pass on the small ray of sunshine before the sun caught up with him again. He looked around and began to panic: he couldn't see Chipmunk.

"Down here!" shouted Chipmunk.

To his relief, he saw Chipmunk's head sticking out of a hole in a large log. Coyote swerved and threw the small ray of sunshine. It arched into the air, spreading light as it flew towards Chipmunk, who was holding out his paws. When it was within reach Chipmunk caught it. Holding it tightly, Chipmunk disappeared into the log and Coyote watched as the light from the small ray of sunshine faded. Chipmunk soon reappeared at the other end of the log and started running towards Squirrel's hiding place. The sun realized Chipmunk now had her small ray of sunshine and started to chase him.

Chipmunk wove in and out of the tall grass, under bushes and around them. He'd seen what had happened to Eagle and Coyote, so tried to keep to the shadows so the sun couldn't catch him. But just as he thought he'd escaped, three rays of sunshine touched Chipmunk's back and it started to get warm. The warmth became a glowing heat, then the heat began to sting. He looked over his shoulder and saw he now had stripes down his back. Just then Squirrel dropped down from a tree and Chipmunk breathed a sigh of relief as he gave the small ray of sunshine to Squirrel. Squirrel held on tightly to it and scampered back up the tree. From branch to branch she leapt. Then from one tree to another, trying to keep to the shadows so the sun couldn't catch her. But just as Squirrel thought she'd outrun the sun she felt her tail becoming warm. The warmth began to turn into a glowing heat, then the heat began to sting. She looked over her shoulder and the heat had curled her tail over. Squirrel began to panic, so she looked around, desperately searching for Mouse. Suddenly she spotted two tiny paws sticking out from a tiny crack at the base of a tree.

"Down here!" Mouse shouted, waving frantically.

Squirrel threw the small ray of sunshine and Mouse managed to catch it. The sun realized Mouse now had her small ray of sunshine, so stopped chasing Squirrel and started to chase Mouse.

Mouse took the small ray of sunshine deep into the tree and started to look for a good hiding place for the small ray of sunshine. The sun tried to follow Mouse with her rays of sunshine, but it didn't matter how hard she tried, she just couldn't reach Mouse. The sun then noticed the moon had begun to rise into the sky and realized she had no choice but to give up.

Not realizing the sun had given up, Mouse hid the small ray of sunshine deep in the knotted roots of the tree, so even he couldn't get it out. And it's still there today. This is why trees burst into flames when hit by lightning, why they burst into flames when it's very hot and why when you rub two sticks together, you get fire.

• • •

Dear Reader

Thank you for buying and reading this book.

We hope you enjoyed this collection of Coyote stories. If you have, would you mind leaving a quick review on Amazon? As an indie publisher reviews help readers find us and our books.

Thank you from the Mad Moment Media team.

To find out about our other books please visit us at:
www.madmomentmedia.com

BIBLIOGRAPHY

Whilst looking for inspiration for the stories in this book the author read the following books.

Afro-American Folk Lore – Tales Told Around Cabin Fires on the Sea Islands of South Carolina collected by A.M.H. Christensen
J.G. Cupples Company (1892)

Folk-Tales of Salishan and Sahaptin Tribes collected by James A. Teit, Marian K. Gould, Livingston Farrand, Herbert J. Spinden and edited by Franz Boas
The American Folk-Lore Society (1917)

In The Reign of Coyote – Folklore From the Pacific Coast by Katherine Chandler
Ginn & Company (1905)

The Mythology of The Wichita collected under the auspices of the Carnegie Institution of Washington by George A. Dorsey
The Carnegie Institution, Washington (1904)

Traditions of the Arikara collected under the auspices of the Carnegie Institution of Washington by George A. Dorsey
The Carnegie Institution, Washington (1904)

ABOUT THE AUTHOR

Lynne started writing professionally in 1997; mainly for UK-based magazines. Since that time, she has had over 25 books and more than 300 features published. Her books have been published in UK, USA, Canada, Holland, Australia, Korea and Indonesia. Her first picture book, *A Book For Bramble*, has been translated into five languages, whilst her second book, *The Best Jumper*, was recorded and aired on the BBC's CBeeBies radio channel.

To learn more about Lynne and her work visit:
www.lynnegarner.com

To find out more about Coyote and his friends, and to keep up to date with all their news please like the author's Facebook page.

www.facebook.com/lynnegarnerauthor

OTHER BOOKS AVAILABLE NOW

Anansi The Trickster Spider
Ten Tales of Brer Rabbit

BOOKS COMING SOON

Hedgehog of Moon Meadow Farm
Fox of Moon Meadow Farm

www.facebook.com/madmomentmedia
www.madmomentmedia.com

Made in the USA
Columbia, SC
19 March 2018